the runaway puppy

Sarang Dev Murthy
Art by Bindia Thapar

ΦKATHA

Once there was a little puppy. He was white all over. Except for his ears which were black. He loved to yelp and jump! He loved to roll and wag his tail.

He loved to lick. He licked the fence. He licked the gate. He licked his mother. He licked anyone and anything he could find.

He had so many brothers and sisters. They had a great time!

One day someone left the small white gate open.
Creak! Creak! the gate went in the wind.
Crea …. kkkkk!

All the pups were scared. They thought the gate was bad and mean.

But the little puppy was curious. He went to find out what was going on! He sniffed at the gate. Then he peeped outside.

He saw a road and cars rushing past!

He saw bicycles with tinkling bells.

And little boys and girls!

He even saw other dogs! What fun! He ran out along the road.

He sniffed here.
He sniffed there.
He sniffed at flowers and bees
and all that he could see.

He sniffed at an old shoe someone had thrown away.

He chased a squirrel all the way up a big tree. The squirrel scampered into a hole in the tree.
 The little puppy sat and waited. And waited for the squirrel to come down.

At last he got tired. He was hungry and thirsty. He wanted his mother. But … where was he? Where was the white gate? And his brothers? His sisters?

Suddenly, he heard a roar. VR ooo OOOM!

A big red truck rumbled past, so close, so very close! Little Puppy jumped. Right into a big ditch.

How safe it was. For a little while he lay there, panting. Then he remembered he was hungry. And thirsty.

He tried to jump out of the ditch. He tried and he tried. But the ditch was too deep! The road was so far away.

Little Puppy started to cry. But no one heard him. He was all alone.

Soon he saw the stars in the sky. They twinkled at him but they were too far to help. The Moon too seemed to want to help. But was too, too far away.

Little Puppy cried and cried till he fell asleep.

The next day a little boy came walking to school on the same road.

He whistled.

He kicked some stones.

He stopped to talk to a little squirrel that he knew. He was thinking about cricket. And his nice new teacher.

Suddenly he heard a sound.

He looked around.

He looked behind him.

He looked to his left and then to his right.

He looked behind the tree.

Then he saw the ditch.

Down he went on his knees. And there was Little Puppy looking up, wagging his tail, barking.

The boy jumped into the ditch. He gently took Little Puppy up and put him softly on the ground.

Lick, lick, lick, went Little Puppy. Licking the boy all over his face.

"Don't do that again!" said the little boy to the puppy, laughing.

He thought the puppy looked hungry. He opened his lunch box and gave it to the puppy.

Then the boy pulled the cap off his water bottle and poured out some water into the cap. Little Puppy ate and drank as if he had never eaten or drunk water before!

"Okay, Ta-ta!" said the little boy, tickling Little Puppy under his chin.

He started walking to school. But the puppy was following him, wagging his tail.

"Go back! Shoo! Go back!" he said. But Little Puppy didn't want to hear. And he went to school too. "Sit outside," said teacher. "And no disturbing the children!" So Little Puppy sat outside. Looking at the butterflies and the birds. Chasing the squirrels. Barking at the cheeky crows.

When school finished, the boy came out. And there was Little Puppy jumping all around him, happy to see him.

At last they reached home.

But now what? How could he keep the puppy? Papa and Amma would not let him, would they? He had asked them before and they had said "No!"

He ran quietly inside and got some biscuits and water. For his new friend.

Next day, Amma said with a smile, "Our son's new teacher must be nice. See how early he is off to school!"

Papa smiled. "Good!"

So it was from that day on. He was up early. He left for school early. And, his lunch box came empty. "Every day!" said Amma with another big smile.

"Ah-ha," said his father proudly. "So you like school, do you?"

The boy grinned. "I like it this much!" he said. "I want to go on Saturday and Sunday, too!"

That is strange, thought his mother.

"Very strange," said Papa.

One day his mother peeped out of the window and saw the little boy's secret! Saw her son and the little puppy romping around. Sharing the sandwich from the lunch box.

So THAT'S what's going on! she thought.

That night, as the little boy slept, his mother went quietly out of the house. Quietly she picked up the puppy and whispered something into his ears. The puppy was delighted. He wagged his tail and agreed to do whatever she told him.

She put him in a big brown cardboard box. And she made lots and lots of holes in it. Then she put the box under the little boy's bed! "Shhhh," she said. "You'll keep the secret, won't you?"

The puppy was very excited but he didn't make a sound all through the night.

The next day came bright and early.

"Happy Birthday!" said the mother, early in the morning. "Happy Big Boy!" she said.

"I'm SIX years old!" shouted the boy, jumping up and down in bed.

His father and mother gave him a hug and plenty of kisses!

"Here's a present for you!" said his father, and he gave him the cardboard box. It was heavy. What was in it?

He opened the box slooooowly and ...

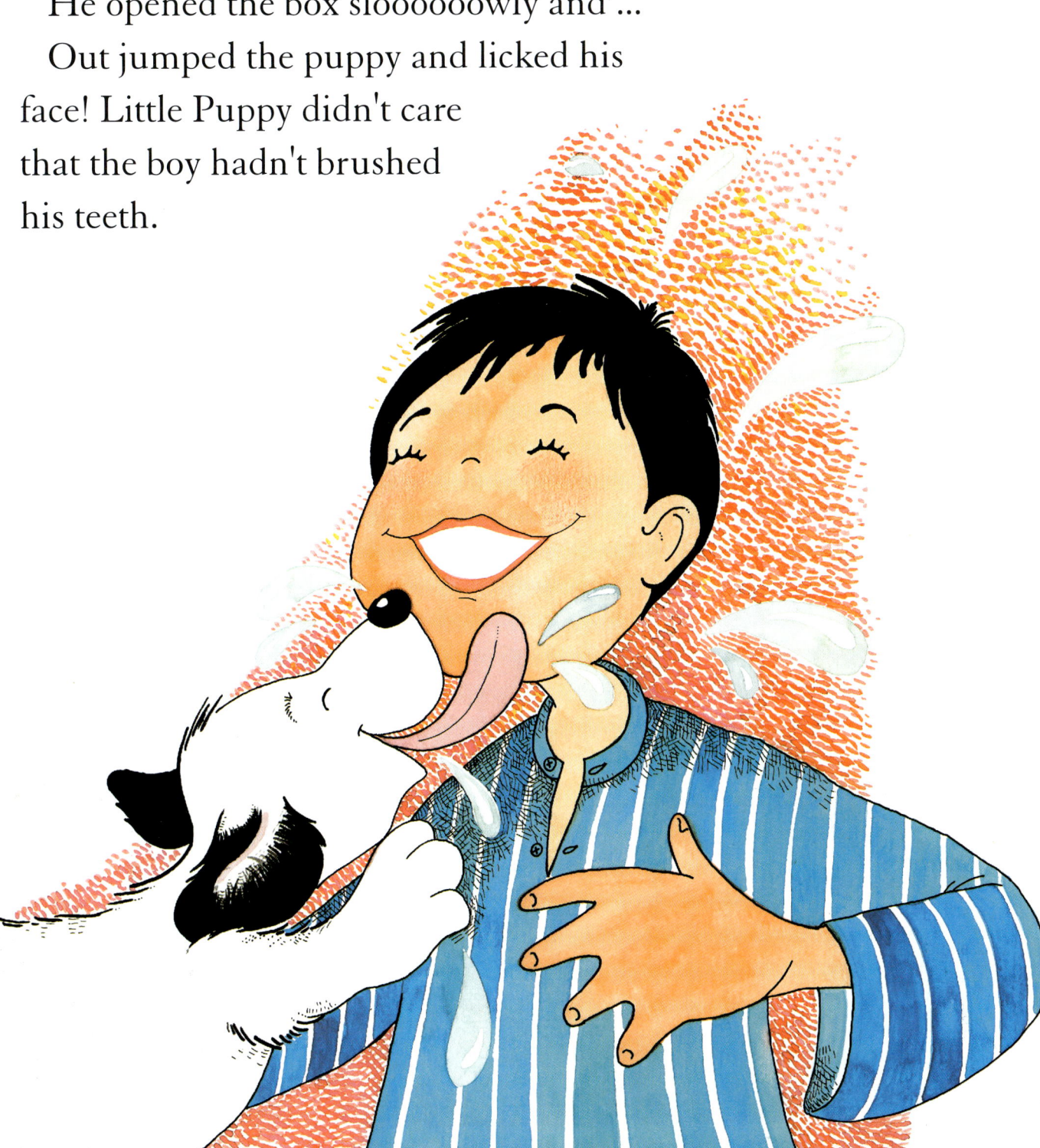

Out jumped the puppy and licked his face! Little Puppy didn't care that the boy hadn't brushed his teeth.

The boy laughed. The puppy barked and wagged his tail. The boy's mother and father laughed too.

"Thank you Amma!" said the boy, hugging his mother. "Thank you Papa!"

It was the best birthday present he had EVER had!

Tamasha Says

Puppies can be a lot of fun. But they need love and care too. Here's what you can do.

- Take your new puppy to an animal doctor. She will tell you how to take care of your friend. And will give her all the vaccinations. These shots will keep your friend healthy and happy.
- Like human babies, puppies feel lost without their mothers. So you must pet her. And talk to her.
- Keep her warm in winter. And cool in summer.
- Puppies need a lot of rest.
- Puppies and dogs feel pain like you. Pick them up gently. Never pick a puppy by her front legs or neck.
- Be nice to your puppy. And you will have the best friend you can ever have!

Make sure your puppy gets her immunization shots regularly.

Try to understand your puppy's language. She can tell you a lot.

Make sure she has a nice, warm and safe place to sleep in. Sweet dreams, puppy!

There's nothing as happy as a fresh, clean puppy. Brush her regularly.

Try not to leave your puppy alone for a long time. She might get into trouble!

You and your puppy both need a balanced and nutritious diet. Eat healthy! Remember - NO SALT, SUGAR OR SPICES in your puppy's diet.